This book belongs to

_____

Nick Sharratt
Splash Day!

Barrington Stoke

First published in 2018 in Great Britain by
Barrington Stoke Ltd
18 Walker Street, Edinburgh, EH3 7LP

www.barringtonstoke.co.uk

Text & Illustrations © 2018 Nick Sharratt

A CIP catalogue record for this book is available
from the British Library upon request

ISBN: 978-1-78112-827-5

Printed in China by Leo

This book is in a super readable format for young readers
beginning their independent reading journey.

This book is dedicated to
the children and staff at
Downs Infant and Junior Schools.

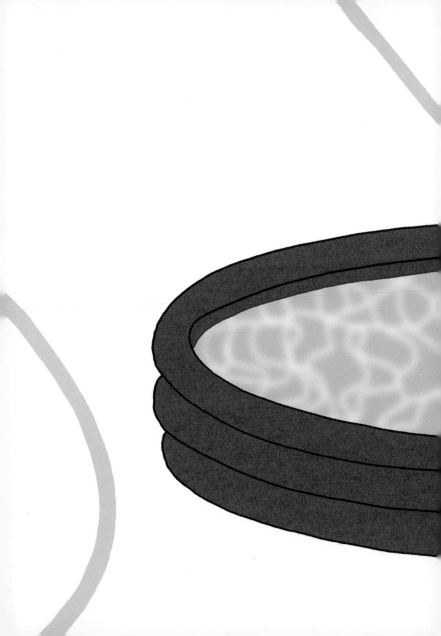

There's a paddling pool in the playground.

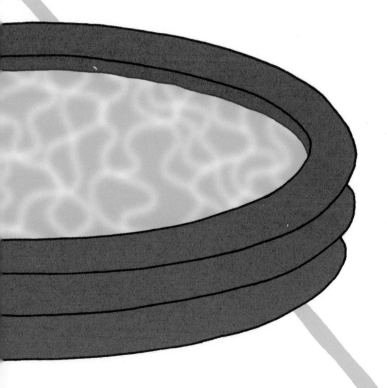

There are washing-up bowls in the goals.

There are crates near the
climbing frame,

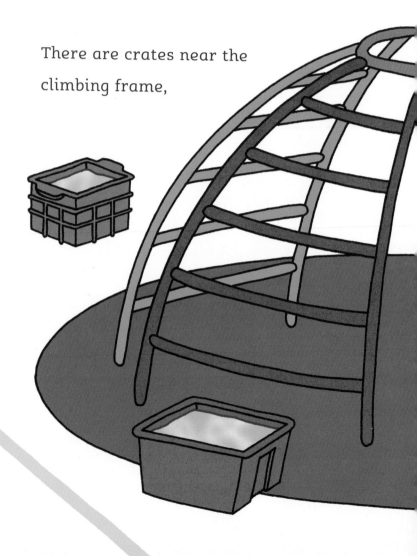

buckets round the bushes,

a sand tray alongside the sunflowers.

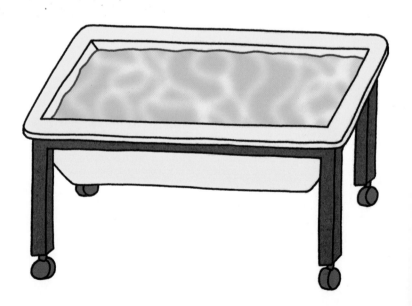

And they're all filled with water.

WHAT'S GOING ON?

Well ... Everyone's worked really hard this year

in English

and Maths

and History

and Art and Design

and Science

and Geography

and P.E.

and Music.

So as a reward ...

Hip Hip
Hooray

It's
Splash Day
today!

Here comes Class One.

Toby's in trunks.

Tilly's in a T-shirt.

William's in a wetsuit.

Soraya's in a swimsuit.

Dev's wearing a diving mask.

And Gabby's wearing goggles.

Hang your towels on
the climbing frame.

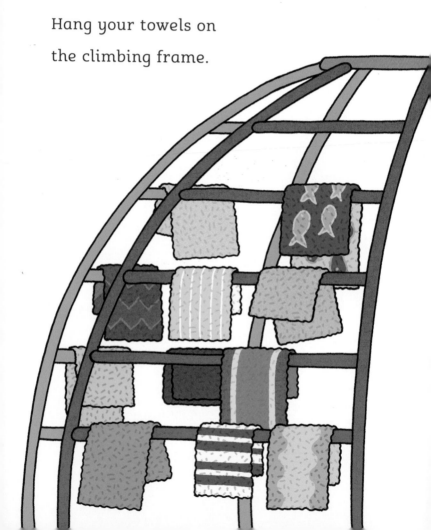

Here come the teachers.

Mrs Poole wears a kagool.

Miss Kelly's wearing wellies.

Mrs McQueen wears a wetsuit that's green.

Mr Flack wears a wetsuit that's black.

Mrs Mapp wears a shower cap.

And Mr Ling wears a rubber ring!

Mrs Thistle blows her whistle.

"Remember please,
no aiming at the face
and under the tree
is a water-free safe place.

Let the water fight begin!"

Everyone runs to fill their water guns,

their pistols and spurters

and sprayers and squirters.

Their sponges and bottles and buckets.

Eek! Squeak! Shriek!

Splosh splash splish!

Eek! Squeak! Shriek!

Splash splish splosh!

Eek! Squeak! Shriek!

Peeeeep!

Everyone stops.

They're all dripping and dropping

and plipping and plopping

and puffing and panting

and gasping and laughing.

Time to get dry.

Let's head for the towels ...

And that's when the head teacher
Mrs Rose comes into the playground
with a hose.

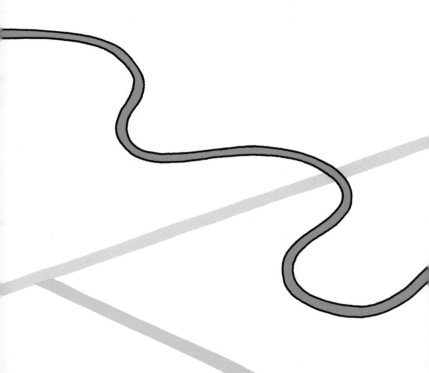

WHHHHOOOOOO

OSSSHHHHH!!!!!!!!

*This story was inspired
by an actual Splash Day
that takes place each year
at a school in Brighton.*

Our books are tested
for children and young people by
children and young people.

Thanks to everyone who consulted on
a manuscript for their time and effort in
helping us to make our books better
for our readers.